THE YOUNG EDITOR
AN ILLUSTRATED BOOK OF FICTION FOR TEENS
BY P.A.KING,Th.D.

ISBN:

Dedicated to All BahamianYouths.no matter your background, Remember that you can become whatever you want to become in life, just put your mind to it and work hard.

THIS BOOK BELONGS TO:

____

BUYER NAME:

THE NASSAU INFORMER DAILY

ZION THE EDITOR

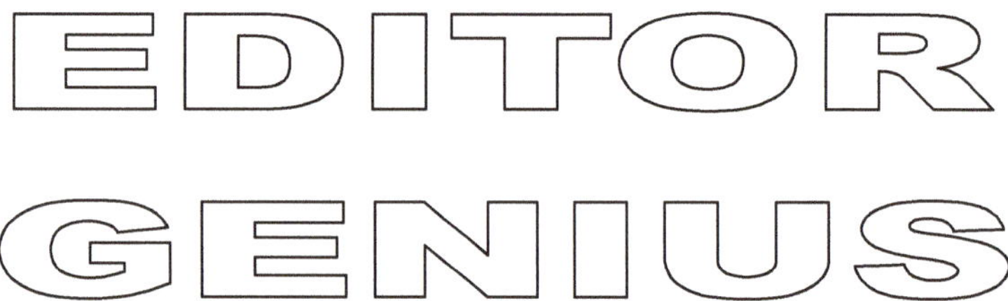

Thief Caught

Iron Bars For Criminal

ROBBER

JAILED

MINISTER AND

POLICE COMMISSIONER

BOAST

<u>FROM THE AUTHOR</u>

Zion had an idea to start a newspaper with his sisters. Clarissa and Zoe. After all writing was in his genes. His uncle princey being an author and all. Never in his wildest dreams could he have imagined that this idea would blossom; better yet mushroom into a flourishing business and help the police solve a crime that had seemed to be archived as a cold case. This would make him famous overnight. Only he didn't know it.

It is hoped that this story of fiction will be used to inspire the author and journalist inside of kids everywhere

Prince Albert King Sr.

The Nassau Informer FRONTPAGE

EDITOR IN CHIEF
ZION DEMERITTE
SATURDAY 30TH APRIL 2020
55CENTS

CRIME NEWS   SPORTS   WEATHER

The Nassau Informer TNI news

NEWS FROM

THE STREETS

OF

NEWPROVIDENCE

Island

Nassau, Bahamas.

POLICE BAFFLED BY INNER CITY THEFT BY ZION DEMERITTE

SOUTH BEACH PROWLER STRIKES AGAIN. GOODS MISSING FROM CLEARS DRYGOODS STORE. A REEWARD OF 200.00 BEING OFFERED FOR INNFORMATION LEADING TO THE ARREST AND CONVICTION OFSUSPECT/S. CONTD. SEE **PAGE 3** POLICE HOLDS PRESS BRIEFING

SEASON 2 BASKETBALL

SOUTH BEACH SPURS VS NASSAU VILLAGE CREW GAME 3-0 SPURS WIN FIRST GAME

PASTORS VS POLITICIANS GAME 4-0 PASTORS WINNING SECOND GAME OF SEASON

VOLLEYBALL L.W.YOUNG EAGLES VS DORIS JOHNSON MARLINS GAME 3-0 EAGLES WIN

A.M MOIST & WET

AFTERNOON SUNSHINE MID 70'S low 69° TOMMORROW 90'S low 85° FINE & SUNNY GOOD DAY FOR THE BEACHES

OTHER NEWS

NEW BAKERY OPENS

THERE IS ANEW BUSINESS IN THE SOUTH BEACH DISTRICT. YOU KNOW HOW WE BAHAMOANS LIKE NEW THINGS. VISIT THE MOSES FOR SOME DELICIOUS DESERTS, COOL DRINKS AND GREAT SERVICE AT AN AFFORDACBLE PRICE; .DO MENTION THIS AD FOR YOUR SPECIAL DISCOUNT. LOCATED ON KENDAL AVENUE, THE STORE IS OWNED BY MS.MARY MOSES

CLASSIFIED ADS

JOB VACANCIES

LOCAL BAKERY SEEKS SALES CLERK – JANITOR-DELIVERY DRIVER BAHAMIANS ONLY NEED APPLY.
1 CREOLE SPEAKING GREETER
1 SPANISH SPEAKING GREETER WAITRESS
APPLY ONLINE:
WWW.BAKERYJOBS@TNI.COM

BAKING CHALLENGE

SAT NOV 21 2020 –R.M.BAILEY SPORTS PARK – BAKE SALE-IN AID OF SCHOOL P.T.A.COMPUTER LAB FUND DRIVE

Chapter one

It was a very boring day. Zion, his sisters Zoe and Clarissa were entertaining a cousin Taniqua who had come to visit for a few days. All of the games were played already. There was nothing else to do. In front of him was a copy of the guardian242newspaper.He glanced at the headline "Another shop break-in" thief on rampage in south beach district. Then it hit him, he should start a newspaper of his own. Yes! He could ask his sisters to help him with this project. It would be something for them to do. This made Zion very excited in deed. His mind became flooded with ideas, on how to lay out the newspaper. I will inform the people of news as it happens. I know what the name will be. I'll call it "The Nassau Informer". There must be a front page for the headlines. Then divide it into Columns. Topics! What can I put in; "I know! He glances at the paper in front of him. Thinking out loud.

Crime, sports, community page, editorial, business section, Ads! " Yeah we could make money to sustain the business from advertisements we need a sales and marketing section". "How about religion and death announcements? A section for fashion, hair and beauty and a section for recipes.

Zion remembered that uncle prince had a print set in the guest bedroom, where he had last stayed a week ago. He was sure if he acted in good faith, that his uncle would not mind him using it, especially if his project was a success. After his entire uncle was a motivator of entrepreneurship. Zion broke the news to the girls. All agreed and with an old fashion hand shake the business was launched. They were in the newspaper business. Just like that." Time for a staff meeting" said Zion. "I want Zoe to record the minutes under the date time place everyone here gets a copy. Zoe will be our secretary for the company. Everyone will go out to gather news stories for today. Interview anyone who would take time out to answer questions.at least try for ten people. The radio was buzzing about a number of shop breaking and stealing reports in south beach. We will start with this story as our main headliner. Sporting events the weather forecast. Also interview every store owner and employee and every policeman on the street if possible. Zion closed the meeting after there were no questions. All present said they understood what was required of them. "Ok everyone time to go out. Get the stories. Remember the WHO, WHAT, WHERE, WHY, HOW take twenty copies to sell on the streets including myself. We will be back here at 12:00noon.All stories will be compiled, edited, proofed read three times then printed. Everybody then left on street assignment.

Main while police had their hands full with another reported shop breaking complaint.

JUSTICE PREVAILS

THE PRINTS FIT YOU MUST CONVICT

NABBED!
TERROR BEAST CAGED!
CASE SOLVED!
BOY HERO!
CITY SAFE AGAIN
POLICE GET THEIR MAN
BOY GENIUS SAVES CITY
POLICE AND MEDIA
PARTNERSHIP CLOSES CASE
SIGH OF RELIEF FOR PUBLIC

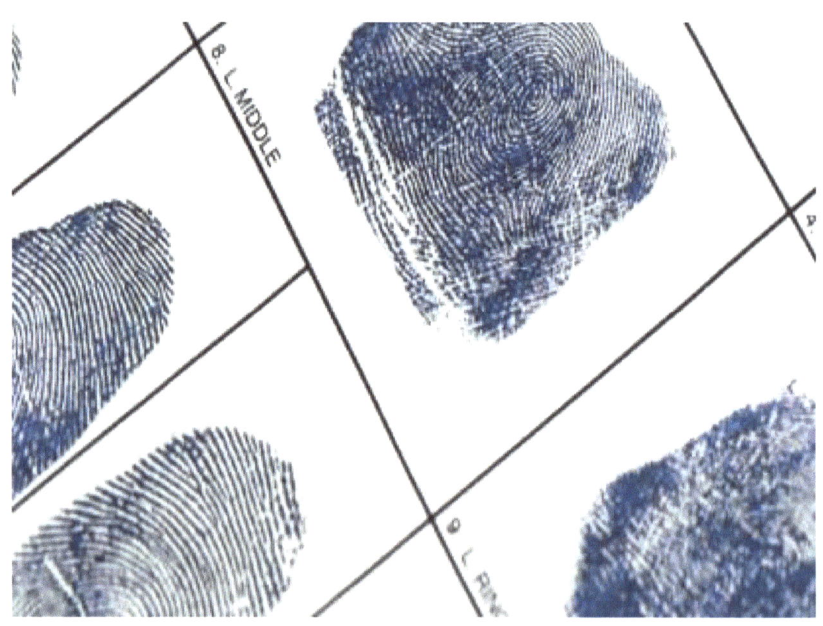

LOOP
ARCH
WHORL

<u>TNI NEWS</u>
Commissioner Ellison Greenslade
holds press brief.

Fingerprints found at scene of one of the shop breakings. Police following several leads.

Down town Nassau

The Commissioner of Police in a statement at today's press conference at Police headquarters said" we are following several leads and there have been fingerprints recovered at the scene of the crime by detectives. This he said would refute claims that the police were baffled and clueless in the cases of the South beach shop breakings as reported by one daily newspaper. These prints could lead to the identity of the culprit/s involved and we hope to come back to you very, very soon with a conclusion to these matters". He added" the royal Bahamas police force always get our man; after all we have a record of say 90 0/0 Ninety percent detection rate. The force has been placed on twelve hour shifts until the crimes are solved and all office staff of all ranks is on the streets".

Following the Commissioner's press briefing. The Police Staff association President Mr. S. Sands made a press statement to protest the long hours of up to some cases 14 hours and outstanding overtime payment situation.

This newspaper and its editor have called for the dedicated officers of the force and their families to continue to give service above self for their beloved country until the payment situation is resolved.

We also call on the powers that be to look into the long overdue pay rise for our men and women in blue as they have promised. The police are working hard on operations, to round up the usual suspects in hopes of finding a match to the prints that were lifted at the scene

Of the crime. The streets are crawling with Police officers, at least two on every main street. The citizenry should feel very safe tonight. We salute our hardworking officers. You must catch this criminal tonight. He belongs behind bars. I challenge no double dog dare you all to leave no stone unturned until he is off the streets. We the citizens will not be afraid, because we are our brother's keepers. Pray for our police.

Editorial by
Zion Demeritte.

The team did their on road assignments. Everyone raced back to the office with their reports. The paper had to be prepared and printed. Everyone was excited. Zion was the most excited! "my name in lights! A self-made editor in one day! He had already started to make plans for his weekly venture of the city's newest newspaper. The papers sheets were laid out, edited and proofed. Zion triple checked every detail with dictionary at hand as if with a fine tooth comb. He gave the signal and mass printing began of fifty copies for sale for starters. "Ok staff back to the streets to sell the papers! Zion shouted. Everyone rushed to the door. All except Zion who wanted to catch the headlines of the radio news. After the headlines were announced he left with his share of the newspapers. Zion headed for Bay and East Streets. He stood on the curbside, waved a paper and shouted" extra extra! Today's news, Read all about it. People passed by rushing along ignoring him as they went on their busy scheduled. One sale came. Zion decided to change his pitch saying" IF IT AIN'T IN THE NASSAU INFORMER, IT AIN'T HAPPENED YET IN NASSAU! People begin to stop and out of curiosity they begin buying the papers until he was sold out. As soon as Zion and crew arrived back to base at the Demeritte's home he knew there was trouble. He could hear voices in the front room. He peeked through the door. There was mom and dad with uncle prince and several neighbors'. Zion said a shy Good Evening to which Uncle Prince said" that's my boy, my nephew the risk taker I am very proud of you! A neighbor said to dad "there is your son who goes about asking people questions and putting their words in the grapevine newspaper of his. People are all talking about it. About what? Said mom "here it is! Said dad holding up one of the copies. Zion Charles Demeritte! What is this about? Said dad. Sir, I just reported what I have seen and heard" I would always introduced myself and the newspaper first before an interview. We only interviewed adults with their consent. Before dad could respond; there was a knock on the door. Uncle Prince went to check. There was no one there; But an envelope with note left inside, that read" because of you being so nosy, the police are on my tail. They cannot catch me because my prints are not in their system. Never been lock up before. I will get you, on the streets little boy! Dad called the police at 911 and made the report. A cruiser that was nearby picked up the radio message. While enroot to the Demeritte's house the officers being vigilant stopped a likely suspect wearing a blue pants and red shirt male five feet nine inches tall dark complexion. The officers called in for a name check. While doing so a neighbor just happened to call the police control room to report a suspicious male of same description putting something in the door of the Demeritte's home and running away in a westerly direction. The Commissioner of police who is always listening to his radio intercepted the call and asked to communicate with the cruiser that had the suspect. He instructed the Officers to take the suspect to the nearest station while another car would be sent to the Demeritte's home to record statement and retrieve the envelope as evidence. And just like that the police had their man. The suspect gave his name as john brown age 25yrs he is visiting folks from one of the family islands. He arrived about two weeks ago. The Commissioner contacted the public defender's office so that an attorney could be present during the interview of the suspect who later confessed writing his own confession under caution. Police officers went door to door to search for witnesses who might have seen the suspect anywhere during the last two weeks day or night. Over twenty witnesses gave statement placing the suspect in areas that were hit during his shop breaking rampage. The suspect cooperated fully with the Police, Attorney general's office and public defender. An identification parade was held in the presence of two judges (retired) and the public defender for impartiality with other suspects of similar height and built, complexion and clothing the next day. All witnesses pointed out the accused it was an iron clad case, the police did great police work not relying on the confession alone. Open and shut. The judges and the public sung their praises for their due diligence. The men and women in blue truly always got their man. That record of fact was still intact thanks to the partnership of the editor, public and the police.

Zion and team were invited to the Paul H. Farquharson conference center at police headquarters for a press brief held by the Commissioner of Police and Minister of National Security. Everyone, in top society was there. Senior Police Officers, Politicians, Past Commissioners of Police and Top journalist all was wanting to pose for a photograph with the boy editor and his team. The Nassau informer was going places. Zion had his names in lights. He became famous overnight as every newspaper in the region told his story. A grand reception was held later on at Government house where Zion received the Governor Generals award for his act of courage in standing up to the criminal FEARLESSLY.

Because of you being so nosy,

the police are on my tail.

They cannot catch me

because my prints are not in their system.

Never been lock up before. You

I will get you, on the streets little

BOY! You Dead already!!

bang! Bang!

STOLEN GOODS RECOVERED

BOY EDITOR SOLVES CRIME

CITY SAFE AGAIN

SOUTH BEACH QUIET, PROWLER REVEALED

it's a match

iron clad confession

THE NASSAU INFORMER

THE NASSAU GUARDIAN

LETTER THREATS FROM PROWLER TO BOY EDITOR LINKS FINGERPRINT MATCH

THE TRIBUNE

FINGERPRINT FITS YOU MUST CONVICT SAYS JUDGE TO JURY

THE PUNCH

CONVICTED!

DOORS SLAMMED

ON

SHOPBREAKER

Now on amazon.com EBOOK (KINDLE) AND PAPERBACK VERSIONS AVAILABLE

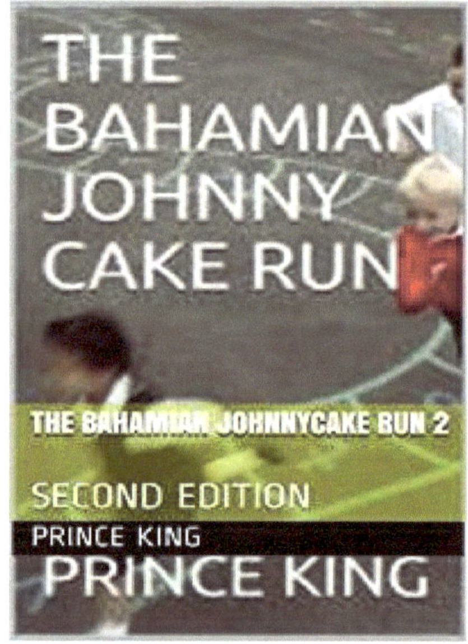

THE LAST OGRE

A CHILDREN'S ILLUSTRATED FAIRY TALE

PRINCE KING

THE LAST OGRE

A book for first time readers. I remember the anxiety that I had experienced at the age of five on the first day of school. And so I decided to write this book to help other kids to see that it isn't all that bad. The character is a little boy who attends school for the first time you have to Trust someone at some time in your life. There are good people in the world, which would not judge you because you are different; but will accept people for who they are. P.A.King

NOW AVAILABLE ON AMAZON.COM

**COMING SOON SUMMER 2020
BOOK2 CHICKCHARNEY FOREST THE
QUEEN SOPHIE RETURNS**

ABOUT THE AUTHOR

Dr. Prince Albert King, Th.D. is a Bahamian author who lives in Nassau, New Providence; He has his roots on Cat Island, Bahamas. He is the author of over thirty books of various genres and a third generation police officer. He is married to the beautiful Samantha Wilson King the couple has Four children. The latest being Prince Albert Bryce King Jr. born Friday April 17th 2020.